Jeremy Jackrabbit's Jumping Journey

by Barbara deRubertis • illustrated by R.W. Alley

THE KANE PRESS / NEW YORK

Alpha Betty's Class

Alexander Anteater

Bobby Baboon

Corky Cub

Dilly Dog

Eddie Elephant

Frances Frog

Gertie Gorilla

Hanna Hippo

Izzy Impala

STAR of the BOOK

Jeremy Jackrabbit

Kylie Kangaroo

Lana Llama

Maxwell Moose

Library of Congress Cataloging-in-Publication Data

deRubertis, Barbara.
Jeremy Jackrabbit's jumping journey / by Barbara deRubertis ; illustrated by R.W. Alley.
p. cm. — (Animal antics A to Z)
ISBN 978-1-57565-321-1 (library binding : alk. paper) — ISBN 978-1-57565-314-3 (pbk. : alk. paper)
[1. Jeremy Jackrabbit discovers that doing what jackrabbits do best—jumping—will help him
overcome jitters and, perhaps, win a trip to Japan. 2. Jumping—Fiction. 3. Jackrabbits—Fiction.
4. Contests—Fiction. 5. Anxiety—Fiction. 6. Animals—Fiction. 7. Alphabet.
8. Humorous stories.] I. Alley, R. W. (Robert W.), ill. II. Title.
PZ7.D4475Jer 2010
[E]—dc22   2009049885

1 3 5 7 9 10 8 6 4 2

First published in the United States of America in 2010 by Kane Press, Inc.
Printed in the United States of America
WOZ0710

Series Editor: Juliana Hanford
Book Design: Edward Miller

Animal Antics A to Z is a registered trademark of Kane Press, Inc.

www.kanepress.com

Jeremy Jackrabbit had always enjoyed jumping rope.

When he was just a little jackbunny, he could jump rope ten times without tripping.

Before long, he could jump a hundred times!

When Jeremy came to Alpha Betty's school, he was a little jittery.

So at recess he decided to do what jackrabbits do best.

He found a jump rope—
and he started to JUMP!

All the kids ran over to Jeremy.
They wanted to be his rope turners!

Jeremy could jump forward,

backward,

and double Dutch.

The other kids were amazed by Jeremy.
"How do you do that?" they asked.

"This is just what jackrabbits do," he joked.
"We jump!"

Soon Jeremy became a little bored with
ordinary jumping.
So he learned to jump on his hands,

on his tail,

and even on his long jackrabbit ears!

"How do you do that?"
the other kids asked.

"This is just what jackrabbits do,"
he joked. "We jump!"

One afternoon Jeremy saw the janitor
putting up a huge sign at school. It said:

Jump Rope
Contest!

Win a Journey to

The Jump Rope
Hall of Fame

in **JAPAN!**

Jeremy's jaw dropped!
"A journey to JAPAN? Jumpin' jellyfish!"

Jeremy jotted down all the details.
Then he jumped home and made a plan.

The next day Jeremy ate a power breakfast.
Carrot muffins with broccoli jam.
And a big jug of lettuce juice.

Then he worked on his jumping.

Jacob Jackal came jogging by.
He was juggling some jingle bells.

Jeremy told Jacob about the contest.
"What would make a jumping jackrabbit
look extra special?" Jeremy asked.

Jacob rubbed his jaw and thought.

"Jazz up your jeans with jingle bells!" he said.
"You'll jingle a jazzy tune while you jump."

Jacob helped Jeremy sew bells on his jeans.
The bells jingled joyfully.

"Jumping in jazzy jeans is even MORE fun!"
cried Jeremy.

Then Jeremy spied Jessica Jaguar playing jacks.
He told her about the jumping contest.

"Let's put jewels on your jacket!" Jessica said.
"Then you'll sparkle while you jump."

They glued jewels all over Jeremy's jacket.
"Now you look jazzy AND jaunty!" said Jessica.

Jeremy's jazzy jeans and jaunty jacket made
him feel extra special.

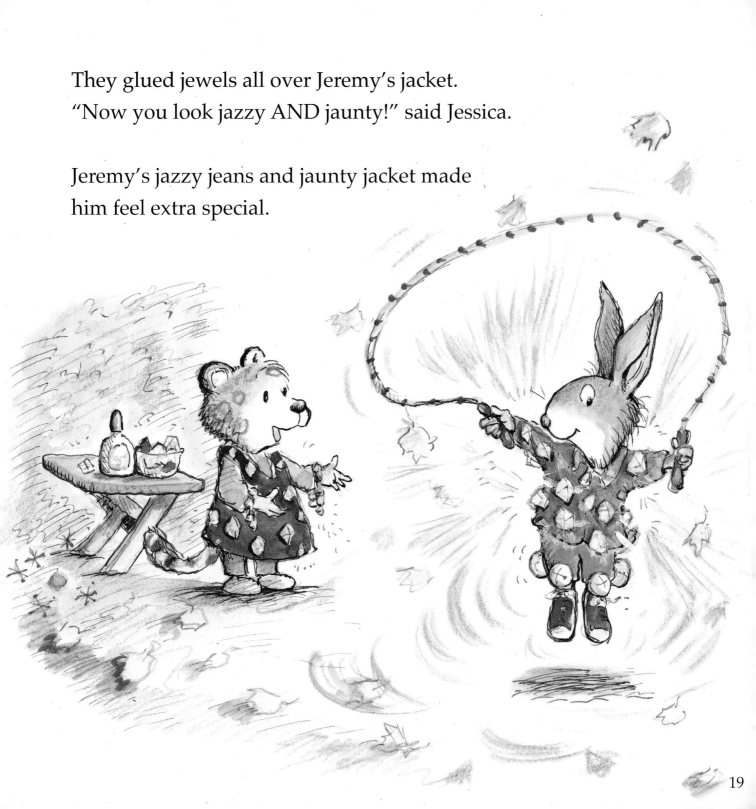

The day of the contest arrived.
Jeremy was last in the long line of jumpers.

He was ready! He would jump faster,
higher, and fancier jumps than ever!

Some of the other jumpers were watching
Jeremy. They were jealous of his jumping.

So they began making fun of him.
"Look at Mr. Jingle-Jangle!" they jeered.

Suddenly Jeremy didn't feel like jumping.

"Don't listen to them," whispered Jacob.
"They're just jealous!"

"Jeremy, just do what you do best!"
said Jessica. "JUMP!"

The judges called Jeremy's name.
He walked over to the jump rope.
His knees felt like jelly.

He tried to keep his jeans from jingling.
But they just jingled and jangled away!

Slowly, Jeremy started to jump.
Jingle! Jangle! Jingle! Jangle!

He looked nervously at the judges.
But the judges were smiling!
Folks in the crowd were smiling, too.

Jeremy started jumping faster. And faster.
And higher. And higher.

His jeweled jacket sparkled.
His jazzy jeans jingled!

And Jeremy did what jackrabbits
do best. He JUMPED!

Jeremy jumped at jet speed.

He was jolly.
He was joyful.
He was jubilant!

Jacob and Jessica started chanting.
"Jump, Jeremy! Jump!
Jump, Jeremy! Jump!"

Soon the whole crowd joined in.
"Jump, Jeremy! Jump!"

The judges leaped to their feet.

"Jeremy Jackrabbit!" they said.
"You are the winner of the journey to Japan!
What is the secret of your success?"

"This is just what jackrabbits do!" Jeremy joked.
"We JUMP!"

And when Jeremy arrived in Japan,
that is exactly what he did.

He JUMPED!

STAR OF THE BOOK: THE JACKRABBIT

FUN FACTS

- **Family:** Jackrabbits are not really rabbits! They belong to the hare family. Hares have longer ears and stronger hind legs than rabbits.
- **Home:** North America—often in deserts, plains, and open spaces
- **Size:** Jackrabbits are about 24 inches long and their ears can grow up to 8 inches long. (Big ears give them excellent hearing.)
- **Food:** More than a pound of grass and plants every day. That's a lot for a 6-pound jackrabbit!
- **Did You Know?** Jackrabbits can run VERY fast—over 40 miles an hour. They can jump 5 feet high and leap as far as 22 feet!

LOOK BACK

Learning to identify letter sounds (phonemes) at the beginning, middle, and end of words is called "phonemic awareness."

- The word *jump* <u>begins</u> with the *j* sound. Listen to the words on page 14 being read again. When you hear a word that <u>begins</u> with the *j* sound, clap your hands once and repeat the word.
- Now listen to the words on page 15 being read again. This time when you hear a word that <u>begins</u> with the *j* sound, pretend you're jumping rope (make a circle with your arms while you jump ONCE) and repeat the word.

TRY THIS!

Stand Up, Sit Down for J Sounds!

- The word *enjoy* is a two-syllable word. It has the *j* sound in the <u>middle</u>. Clap your hands as you say each syllable: *en-joy*.
- Listen while someone reads a two-syllable word in the word bank below. Sit on a chair and clap softly when you repeat the first syllable. Stand up and clap LOUDLY when you repeat the second syllable, the one that begins with *j*.

| major | object | reject | enjoy | rejoice | subject |

FOR MORE ACTIVITIES, go to Jeremy Jackrabbit's website: www.kanepress.com/AnimalAntics/JeremyJackrabbit.html You'll also find a recipe for Jeremy Jackrabbit's Carrot Muffins!